Prologue: The Last Light

The village of Briarhold lay qu
of dusk. A faint mist curled thi
clinging to the thatched rooftops and winding its way around the stone walls that had stood for centuries. To the villagers, the fog was a familiar veil, one that softened the harshness of life in the wilds of Evershade. But tonight, the mist brought with it an unnatural chill, a whisper of danger that set the dogs howling and the horses stamping in their stalls.

Inside the modest chapel at the heart of Briarhold, the only light came from a single candle, flickering in the chill breeze that slipped through the cracks in the old wooden door. Father Mathis knelt before the altar, his lips moving in silent prayer. He had been praying for hours, his heart heavy with the knowledge that something dark was coming. The signs were unmistakable—the livestock falling ill without cause, the sudden silence of the forest, and the ominous blood-red moon that hung low in the sky.

He was not alone in his fear. The villagers had gathered in the small square outside, clutching makeshift weapons and muttering anxiously among themselves. They had heard the stories, passed down from their grandparents and great-grandparents, of the terrible scourge that had once plagued their land: witches, whose black magic could blight the crops, poison the wells, and twist men's minds to madness.

The door of the chapel creaked open, and a young boy, no more than ten, slipped inside. His eyes were wide with fear as he looked at Father Mathis.

"They're here," the boy whispered, his voice trembling.

Father Mathis felt his blood run cold. He rose slowly, his joints aching from hours on his knees. He took the candle from the altar and turned to the boy.

"Gather everyone in the chapel," he said. "We must pray for deliverance."

The boy nodded and ran out, his small footsteps echoing in the silence. Father Mathis followed, his heart pounding. As he stepped outside, he saw them—dark figures moving at the edge of the village, their silhouettes barely visible in the thickening fog. The villagers shouted, brandishing their pitchforks and knives, but the figures did not stop. They moved with an eerie, deliberate grace, their eyes glowing faintly in the darkness.

Father Mathis raised the candle high, the small flame flickering wildly in the night air. "In the name of the Light, I command you to leave this place!" he cried, his voice strong despite the fear that clawed at his throat.

The figures halted, and for a moment, the only sound was the crackling of the candle flame. Then, a soft, mocking laugh echoed through the village. A woman stepped forward, her face hidden beneath the hood of a tattered cloak. She raised her hand, and the flame of the candle flickered once, twice, and then went out.

Darkness fell over Briarhold.

"Your light cannot save you now, priest," the woman said, her voice cold and sharp as broken glass. "We are the daughters of the night, and we have come to reclaim what is ours."

Father Mathis stumbled back, his heart hammering in his chest. The villagers surged forward, but with a wave of the woman's hand, they were thrown back, crashing into the ground as if struck by an invisible force. Panic erupted, screams filling the air as the villagers scrambled to their feet, only to be caught in a web of shadow and fire.

The woman laughed again, and with a flick of her wrist, the chapel burst into flames, the heat searing the night air. The villagers fell to their knees, their eyes wide with terror as the flames rose higher, painting the sky a furious red.

Father Mathis could only watch, his hands trembling, as the woman turned to him, her eyes burning like embers in the darkness.

"Tell your masters," she whispered, her voice echoing with a terrible power, "that the time of the Fire Hunters is over. The witches have returned, and the world will burn."

As the flames consumed the village, a single figure stood at the edge of the forest, watching with cold, calculating eyes. Aric Thorn, the last of the Fire Hunters, clenched his fists, his jaw set in grim determination.

The hunt had begun.

Chapter 1: The Burden of Ashes

Aric Thorn stood on the ridge overlooking what remained of Briarhold, his breath fogging in the cool morning air. The village was little more than a smoldering ruin now, a blackened scar on the landscape. The scent of smoke and charred wood lingered, mingling with the acrid stench of burnt flesh. He had seen such devastation before, too many times to count, but it never failed to twist his gut with a familiar, seething anger.

His hand drifted to the hilt of his sword, the worn leather grip a comforting weight beneath his gloved fingers. The blade, etched with ancient runes that glowed faintly in the early light, was all that remained of the once-great Order of Fire Hunters. It was both a weapon and symbol—a reminder of the oath he had sworn and the lives that had been lost.

He turned away from the wreckage, his eyes scanning the treeline. There were no signs of life, no tracks leading away from the village. The witches had vanished as quickly as they had appeared, leaving only death and destruction in their wake. It was as if they were taunting him, daring him to follow, knowing he was alone and powerless to stop them.

But he would find them. And when he did, he would make them pay.

A rustling sound behind him drew his attention. He spun, his sword flashing free of its sheath in one fluid motion. A figure stepped out from behind a cluster of rocks, hands raised in a gesture of peace.

"Easy there, Hunter," the figure said, her voice low and calm. "I'm not here to fight."

Aric narrowed his eyes, taking in the stranger's appearance. She was young, barely more than a girl, with unruly dark hair that fell around her shoulders and eyes that seemed too old for her face. Her clothes were rough and travel-worn, but her posture was confident, almost defiant.

"Who are you?" he demanded, his grip on the sword tightening.

The girl shrugged, a faint smile playing on her lips. "Name's Elara. I heard what happened here last night. Thought I'd see for myself."

Aric's eyes narrowed further. "And why would you do that?"

Elara's smile widened, but it didn't reach her eyes. "Let's just say I've got a score to settle with the ones who did this."

He studied her for a long moment, searching for any sign of deception. There was something about her that set his teeth on edge, a sense of danger that he couldn't quite place. But there was no time to waste on mistrust. If she knew something that could help him track the witches, he would take the risk.

"Fine," he said at last, sheathing his sword. "But if you try anything—"

Elara rolled her eyes. "You'll what? Kill me? We both know you've got bigger problems than a girl with a grudge."

Aric bit back a retort and turned away, heading down the slope toward the village. Elara fell into step beside him, her movements light and silent. They walked in silence for a while, the only sound the crunch of their boots on the frost-covered ground.

"What do you know about the attack?" he asked finally, his voice gruff.

"Not much more than you, I'd guess," she said, her tone casual. "A new coven moved into Evershade. They've been hitting villages on the outskirts, testing their strength. This is just the beginning."

Aric's jaw tightened. He had feared as much. The witches were growing bolder, more organized. It was only a matter of time before they turned their sights on the larger towns, and then the cities.

"And you're here to help me stop them?" he asked, his voice laced with skepticism.

Elara shrugged again. "I have my reasons. Let's just leave it at that."

He shot her a sidelong glance, his eyes narrowing. There was something she wasn't telling him, but he didn't have the luxury of questioning her motives. Not yet.

They reached the ruins of the chapel, the charred remains still smoldering in the cold air. Aric knelt, sifting through the ash with a practiced hand. He found the remains of a broken amulet, the silver warped and blackened by the flames. He turned it over in his hand, his expression grim.

"This was a ward," he said quietly. "They broke through the defenses like they were nothing."

Elara crouched beside him, her gaze sharp. "Powerful magic. Stronger than anything I've seen in years."

Aric nodded, slipping the amulet into his pouch. He rose, his eyes sweeping over the ruins. "We need to find their lair. Before they strike again."

Elara stood as well, brushing ash from her hands. "I might know someone who can help. A seer, deep in the forest. She's... difficult, but if anyone can track these witches, it's her."

Aric hesitated. Trusting a stranger was bad enough; trusting a seer was worse. But he had no other leads, and time was running out.

"Lead the way," he said finally, his voice hard.

Elara nodded, a strange look crossing her face—something like relief, or perhaps anticipation. She turned and began to walk, her steps quick and sure.

Aric followed, his heart heavy with the weight of the hunt that lay ahead. The witches were gathering their strength, preparing for something terrible. And he was all that stood between them and the innocent lives they sought to destroy.

The fire burned within him, bright and unyielding. He would not rest until every last one of them was ashes at his feet.

The hunt was just beginning.

Chapter 2: The Seer's Price

The path through Evershade Forest was treacherous, even for those who knew its twists and turns. Gnarled roots twisted up from the ground like the fingers of the dead, and thick underbrush threatened to trip the unwary traveler. The dense canopy overhead blocked out most of the sunlight, casting the forest in a perpetual twilight. It was a place of shadows and secrets, where few dared to tread.

Elara moved through the forest with the ease of someone who had spent much of her life navigating its hidden trails. Aric followed her, his eyes scanning their surroundings for any sign of danger. He had heard stories of the creatures that prowled these woods—wolves with eyes of fire, serpents with scales as black as night, and worse things that had no name. But it wasn't the beasts that worried him. It was the silence, a silence so complete it pressed down on them like a heavy shroud. The forest was watching them, waiting.

"Are you sure this seer can help us?" Aric asked, his voice low.

Elara didn't look back as she replied. "As sure as I can be about anything. She's not exactly the friendly sort, but if anyone knows where the witches are hiding, it's her."

Aric grunted in response, not entirely reassured. He had dealt with seers before, and they were rarely straightforward. They spoke in riddles and half-truths, their motives as twisted as the paths they tread. But he had little choice. The witches were growing stronger with each passing day, and he needed answers.

They walked in silence for what felt like hours, the air growing colder and the trees taller and more twisted as they ventured deeper into the forest. At last, they came to a small clearing, dominated by a massive oak tree that towered above them, its branches spreading out like the arms of some ancient, watchful guardian. At its base was a door, barely visible beneath the gnarled roots.

"This is it," Elara said softly, her voice barely more than a whisper. "The Seer of Evershade."

Aric frowned, eyeing the door warily. It was made of rough-hewn wood, ancient and weathered, and seemed to pulse with a faint, unnatural energy. He felt a prickle of unease crawl down his spine.

"What are you waiting for?" Elara asked, raising an eyebrow. "Scared?"

He shot her a glare but said nothing. Taking a deep breath, he stepped forward and knocked on the door. The sound echoed through the clearing, louder than it should have been, and then there was silence.

For a long moment, nothing happened. Then, with a creak, the door swung open, revealing a dark passageway that sloped down into the earth. A chill breeze wafted out, carrying with it the scent of damp earth and something else, something sharp and metallic.

Elara stepped forward, her expression set. "Stay close. And whatever you do, don't speak unless she asks you a direct question."

Aric nodded, his hand resting on the hilt of his sword as they descended into the darkness. The passageway was narrow and winding, the walls close enough to brush his shoulders. Strange symbols were carved into the stone, their meaning lost to time. He could feel the weight of them pressing down on him, a thousand eyes watching from the shadows.

They reached the bottom of the stairs, emerging into a circular chamber lit by a faint, eerie glow. At the center of the room stood a stone pedestal, and on it, a bowl filled with a dark, viscous liquid. The walls were covered in strange markings, and the air hummed with a low, thrumming energy that made Aric's skin crawl.

And there, seated on a low, carved throne, was the Seer.

She was old, impossibly old, her skin thin and pale as parchment, her hair a wild tangle of silver that fell around her like a veil. Her eyes were clouded and white, as if she were blind, but Aric knew better. Those eyes saw everything.

"You've brought a visitor, child," the Seer rasped, her voice a dry whisper like leaves rustling in the wind. "A Fire Hunter, no less. How unexpected."

Elara inclined her head, her posture respectful. "We seek your guidance, Seer. There is a new coven in Evershade. They've already destroyed Briarhold, and they're growing stronger by the day. We need to know where they are."

The Seer tilted her head, her sightless eyes fixing on Aric. He felt a cold shiver run down his spine as her gaze pierced through him, as if she were peeling back the layers of his soul, exposing his every secret.

"And why should I help you, Fire Hunter?" she murmured, a faint smile curling her lips. "What can you offer me that I do not already possess?"

Aric swallowed, struggling to find his voice. He had been prepared for many things, but not for this. He glanced at

Elara, but she gave him no help, her expression unreadable.

"Anything you ask, Seer," he said finally, his voice steady. "If you can help us find the witches, I will repay you however I can."

The Seer chuckled, a dry, rasping sound. "Anything, you say? Be careful with your words, Hunter. They have power here."

She reached out a hand, her fingers trembling with age, and dipped them into the bowl on the pedestal. When she withdrew them, they were stained with the dark liquid, which she smeared across her brow, muttering words in a language Aric did not understand.

"I see a great fire," she whispered, her eyes distant. "A fire that will consume all in its path, unless it is stopped. The witches seek to claim this power, to wield it as their own. But they do not understand. They do not see."

Her voice dropped to a low, almost inaudible murmur. "There is a place, deep in the heart of Evershade, where the veil between worlds is thin. There, the coven gathers, drawn by the promise of power. But beware, Hunter. For not all is as it seems."

She fell silent, her head bowing as if the effort had drained her. Aric waited, his heart pounding in his chest. He knew better than to push her for more. The price for knowledge was often high, and he could not afford to anger her.

"Thank you, Seer," Elara said softly, taking a step back. "We will find them."

The Seer lifted her head, her eyes fixing on Elara with a sudden, fierce intensity. "You, child, walk a dangerous path. The fire within you burns bright, but it could just as easily consume you. Remember that, when the time comes."

Elara stiffened, but she said nothing. She bowed her head, and after a moment, Aric did the same. They turned and left the chamber, the Seer's eyes following them until they disappeared up the stairs and out into the cool forest air.

As they emerged back into the clearing, Aric turned to Elara, his expression grim. "What did she mean by that? The fire within you?"

Elara's face was a mask of indifference, but he could see the tension in her posture. "It's nothing. Old superstitions."

He didn't believe her, but he let it go. They had more pressing matters to attend to.

"Did you understand what she was talking about?" he asked instead. "This place where the veil is thin?"

Elara nodded, her eyes distant. "I think so. There's a grove, deep in the forest. It's... different. The trees there are ancient, twisted. People say it's a place of power, a place where the barrier between our world and the spirit world is weak."

Aric frowned. "And that's where the coven is?"

"Most likely," Elara said. "If they're looking for power, that's the place to find it."

He nodded, his mind already working through the possibilities. The grove would be difficult to reach, even more difficult to approach unnoticed. But if the witches were there, they had no choice.

"We leave at dawn," he said, his voice firm. "We'll find this grove, and we'll end this."

Elara didn't respond, but he could see the determination in her eyes. Whatever her reasons, she was committed to this fight. And for now, that was enough.

As the shadows deepened around them, they made camp at the edge of the clearing, the fire casting long, flickering shadows on the ground. Aric kept watch, his eyes scanning the darkness for any sign of movement. Elara lay on her side, her back to the fire, her breathing slow and even.

But Aric knew she was not asleep. He could feel the tension radiating from her, the sense of something held tightly in check.

He sighed and turned his gaze to the sky, where the stars glittered coldly overhead. The Seer's words echoed in his mind, filling him with a sense of foreboding he could not shake.

The hunt was far from over, and the darkness ahead was deeper and more dangerous than anything he had faced before.

Chapter 3: The Haunted Grove

The dawn came pale and cold, the sun barely a ghostly glow through the thick canopy above. Aric and Elara broke camp in silence, their movements quick and efficient. The air was heavy with anticipation, a sense of urgency driving them forward as they set off deeper into the forest.

The path to the grove was difficult to find, hidden among the twisted roots and tangled undergrowth. Elara led the way, her steps sure despite the treacherous terrain. Aric followed closely, his hand never far from the hilt of his sword. He could feel the air growing colder, a chill that seeped into his bones and made his breath come out in white puffs.

"There it is," Elara said quietly, pointing ahead.

Aric followed her gaze and felt a shiver run down his spine. The grove lay before them, a dark, brooding mass of trees that seemed to huddle together as if whispering secrets to each other. The trunks were thick and gnarled, their bark blackened and twisted, and the branches overhead formed a dense canopy that blocked out the sky. A faint mist clung to the ground, swirling around their feet like a living thing.

"Stay close," Elara murmured, her voice barely audible. "The energy here... it's different. Stronger."

Aric nodded, his eyes scanning the shadows for any sign of movement. The Seer's warning echoed in his mind, filling him with a sense of unease he couldn't shake.

They moved cautiously, their steps silent on the soft earth. The trees seemed to close in around them, their branches reaching down like skeletal fingers. The air was thick with the scent of damp earth and decay, and Aric felt his heart begin to race as they ventured deeper into the grove.

And then he saw it—a faint glow, barely visible through the dense foliage. He signaled to Elara, and they crept closer, their movements slow and deliberate.

As they drew near, the source of the light became clear. A circle of stones stood in the center of a small clearing, each one carved with intricate runes that pulsed with a faint, ethereal glow. In the center of the circle, a figure knelt, her hands raised in supplication as she chanted softly in a language Aric did not understand.

The witch.

He felt a surge of anger and relief. They had found her. But as he started forward, Elara grabbed his arm, her grip surprisingly strong.

"Wait," she whispered, her eyes wide. "There's something wrong."

Aric frowned but held his ground, his eyes locked on the figure in the clearing. The witch continued to chant, her voice rising and falling in a strange, haunting melody. The air around her shimmered, and Aric felt a prickling sensation on his skin, as if the very fabric of reality were being stretched thin.

"What is she doing?" he muttered, his grip tightening on his sword.

Elara's face was pale, her eyes fixed on the witch. "She's opening a portal. But... she's not alone."

Aric's heart skipped a beat. He strained his ears, listening, and then he heard it—a low, rumbling growl that seemed to come from everywhere at once. The ground beneath their feet trembled, and a shape emerged from the shadows, massive and dark.

A creature stepped into the clearing, its eyes glowing with an unnatural light. It was unlike anything Aric had ever seen, its form shifting and indistinct, as if it were made of smoke and shadow. It moved with a terrible grace, circling the witch as she chanted, its eyes never leaving her.

"What is that?" Aric breathed, his voice barely more than a whisper.

Elara shook her head, her expression grim. "A shadow beast. They're guardians of the veil, creatures of pure magic. If she's summoned one, she's more powerful than we thought."

Aric's mind raced. They were outmatched, outnumbered. Charging in now would be suicide. But if they didn't stop her, whatever she was trying to summon would be unleashed upon the world.

He glanced at Elara, his jaw set. "Can you distract the beast?"

She looked at him as if he'd lost his mind. "Are you serious? That thing will tear me apart."

"It's our only chance," he insisted, his voice urgent. "I'll take the witch. You just need to buy me a few seconds."

Elara hesitated, fear and determination warring in her eyes. Then she nodded, her expression hardening. "Fine. But if I die, I'm haunting you."

Aric almost smiled. "I'll take my chances."

He drew his sword, the runes along the blade flaring to life with a soft, blue light. Elara took a deep breath and stepped forward, her hand outstretched. A soft, golden light began to glow in her palm, spreading outwards until it enveloped her entire body.

The shadow beast's head snapped around, its eyes narrowing as it caught sight of the light. With a low, rumbling growl, it turned away from the witch and began to stalk toward Elara, its movements slow and deliberate.

"Hey, ugly!" Elara called, her voice strong and clear. "Come and get me!"

The beast roared, a sound that seemed to shake the very air, and lunged.

Elara dodged to the side, the light around her flaring brightly as she raised her hand. A burst of golden energy shot out, striking the beast in the chest. It staggered, its form flickering like a candle in the wind, but it did not fall.

Aric didn't wait to see what happened next. He sprinted forward, his sword raised. The witch didn't see him until it was too late. With a single, fluid motion, he brought his blade down, severing her chant in a spray of blood.

The witch screamed, a terrible, piercing sound, and the air around them exploded with a burst of raw, chaotic energy.

Aric was thrown back, his vision swimming as he hit the ground hard.

For a moment, everything was a blur. He struggled to his feet, his head spinning, and saw the witch crumpled on the ground, her blood pooling around her. The runes on the stones flickered and died, the portal collapsing with a final, thunderous crash.

The shadow beast roared again, a sound of pure rage, and turned on Aric, its eyes blazing. He raised his sword, bracing himself for the attack.

But before the beast could strike, a blinding flash of light erupted from Elara's outstretched hand, engulfing the creature. It screamed, a sound of agony and fury, and then it was gone, its form dissolving into nothingness.

Elara staggered, her face pale and drawn. Aric rushed to her side, catching her before she could fall.

"Are you all right?" he asked, his voice tight with worry.

She nodded weakly, her breath coming in shallow gasps. "I'm fine. Just... used a bit too much energy."

He helped her to her feet, his eyes scanning the clearing. The witch lay dead, her body twisted and broken. The stones were dark and silent, the magic gone.

"We did it," he murmured, almost in disbelief. "We stopped her."

Elara nodded, her eyes clouded with exhaustion. "For now. But there are others. This is just the beginning, Aric."

He knew she was right. The witch had been powerful, but she was only one of many. The coven was still out there, and they would not stop until they had what they wanted.

But they had won a small victory today, and for now, that was enough.

As they turned to leave the grove, the shadows seemed to shift and stir around them, whispering of secrets yet to be revealed. The hunt was far from over, and the darkness that lay ahead was deep and unfathomable.

But they would face it together. And whatever came next, they would be ready

Chapter 4: The Council of Elders

The journey back to the settlement was tense and silent. The air between Aric and Elara crackled with unspoken thoughts and lingering questions. They arrived under the cloak of darkness, the hidden enclave nestled deep within the heart of the mountains. The Fire Hunters' stronghold was a sprawling network of stone structures and underground chambers, protected by powerful wards and guarded by seasoned warriors.

As they approached the central hall, Aric felt the weight of what they had discovered bearing down on him. The Elders needed to know, but he feared their response. Elara walked beside him, her face set in a mask of determination, though he could see the uncertainty in her eyes.

The Council chamber was an imposing room, its high ceilings and stone walls adorned with ancient banners depicting the history of the Fire Hunters. A large, circular table sat in the center, around which the Elders were already gathered, their faces illuminated by the flickering light of the brazier that burned in the center.

Elder Rylan, the head of the Council, looked up as they entered. His piercing blue eyes, sharp despite his age, fixed on Aric and Elara with an intensity that made Aric's skin prickle. "You've returned," he said, his voice a deep rumble. "Report."

Aric stepped forward, his voice steady. "We found the witch in Evershade, as you suspected. She was performing a ritual, opening a portal to summon a shadow beast. We stopped her, but not before she revealed something troubling."

He glanced at Elara, who took a deep breath before continuing. "She spoke of an artifact, the *Lament of Cindras*. They believe it can break the veil between the spirit world and ours. If they unlock its power, they could unleash chaos on the world."

A murmur rippled through the chamber as the Elders exchanged worried glances. Rylan's expression darkened. "The *Lament of Cindras* is a myth. A legend meant to frighten children."

"Not anymore," Aric said grimly. "We found evidence in the witch's belongings that suggests they're searching for it. They've already made progress."

Elder Malin, a stern woman with silver-streaked hair, leaned forward. "If this is true, then the situation is more dire than we imagined. The witches have never been so bold. What are they planning?"

Aric shook his head. "We're not sure yet. But whatever it is, it's big."

Elara shifted uneasily. "I felt a power in the grove. Something ancient and dark. They're not just hunting for the *Lament*. They're looking for something... more."

The chamber fell silent, the weight of her words settling over them like a shroud. Elder Orin, a quiet, enigmatic figure, finally spoke, his voice soft but carrying a strange resonance. "There is more at play here than we understand. The witches' motives are unclear, but we cannot underestimate them. They are gathering strength, and if they truly believe the *Lament of Cindras* can be found, we must act swiftly."

Rylan nodded, his gaze sweeping the room. "We need more information. Aric, Elara, you are to continue your investigation. Find out what the witches are planning and, if possible, locate the *Lament* before they do."

Elara hesitated, then stepped forward. "Elder Orin, you seemed to know something about my past. About why the witches might be interested in me. I need to understand what's going on."

All eyes turned to Orin, who regarded her with a strange, unreadable expression. "Your past is tied to a lineage of great power, Elara. A power that the witches may seek to exploit. But there is much you do not know, and much that remains hidden, even from me."

Elara's eyes flashed with frustration. "Then tell me what you do know."

Orin's gaze softened. "Your family was once part of a powerful coven, one that was betrayed and destroyed. You carry a legacy of magic within you, a legacy that the witches might see as a threat... or as a tool."

Aric stiffened, his eyes narrowing. "What does that mean for us?"

Orin sighed. "It means that Elara is more than just a Fire Hunter. Her presence alone could draw the witches to her, or even turn the tide in this war. You must be cautious."

Rylan stood, his expression firm. "Enough. We cannot afford to dwell on uncertainties. You have your orders. Find the witches, and stop them. The fate of our world may depend on it."

Aric and Elara exchanged a glance, a silent understanding passing between them. Whatever secrets lay in Elara's past, whatever dangers awaited them, they would face them together. They turned and left the chamber, the weight of their mission pressing down on their shoulders like a storm cloud gathering on the horizon.

Chapter 5: Secrets Unveiled

The cold mountain air bit into Elara's skin as she and Aric made their way back to their quarters. The Council's words echoed in her mind, mixing with the unease that had taken root since the battle in the grove. Aric was silent beside her, his face set in a grim mask. She wanted to reach out, to say something, but the uncertainty between them held her back.

When they reached the small stone building that served as their quarters, Aric finally spoke, his voice tight. "Why didn't you tell me about your family?"

Elara flinched at the accusation in his tone. "I didn't know. Not really. I knew my parents were different, that they had some connection to magic, but they never spoke about it. They died when I was young, and I was taken in by the Fire Hunters. I thought... I thought it was behind me."

Aric's eyes searched hers, and she saw the hurt there, the betrayal. "But you have magic. You've used it."

"Yes," she admitted, her voice barely a whisper. "I've felt it, always, like a fire burning inside me. But I was afraid. Afraid of what it meant, and what would happen if the Fire Hunters found out. So I tried to hide it, even from myself."

Aric shook his head, turning away. "And now the witches are after you because of it. You've put us all in danger."

"I know," she said, her voice breaking. "I'm sorry. I should have told you. But I was scared, Aric. Scared of what I might be, and scared of losing you."

He looked back at her, his expression softening slightly. "Elara..."

She stepped closer, reaching out to touch his arm. "Please, Aric. I need you to trust me. I'm on your side. I want to stop the witches just as much as you do."

He sighed, the tension leaving his shoulders. "I know. It's just... a lot to take in."

Elara nodded, relief washing over her. "We'll figure this out. Together."

Aric managed a small smile. "Together."

The following days were spent in tense preparation. The Council had provided them with a lead: a hidden library in the ruins of an old monastery, where they might find information about the *Lament of Cindras*. It was a dangerous journey, but they had no choice. If the witches found the artifact first, it could mean the end of everything they had sworn to protect.

They set out at dawn, the first light of day casting long shadows across the mountains. The path to the monastery was treacherous, winding through narrow passes and dense forests where dangers lurked in every shadow. But they pressed on, driven by the urgency of their mission.

It was near dusk when they finally reached the crumbling remains of the monastery. The air was thick with the scent of damp stone and ancient dust, and a sense of foreboding hung over the place like a shroud. Elara shivered, drawing her cloak tighter around her shoulders as they made their way inside.

The library was hidden deep within the ruins, accessible only through a series of secret passages that Aric seemed to navigate with ease. Elara followed closely, her senses on high alert. She could feel the pulse of magic in the air, a faint hum that set her nerves on edge.

They finally reached a small, dimly lit chamber filled with shelves of dusty tomes and scrolls. Aric wasted no time, moving to a section labeled with symbols Elara didn't recognize. "These are records of the ancient wars," he explained, pulling out a large, leather-bound book. "If there's any mention of the *Lament of Cindras*, it'll be here."

They spent hours poring over the texts, the silence broken only by the soft rustle of pages turning. It was Elara who finally found it, a passage buried in the middle of a crumbling manuscript. She read aloud, her voice hushed with awe and fear.

"'The *Lament of Cindras*, forged in the fires of despair, sealed with the blood of the innocent. A key to the veil, a weapon against the darkness. It lies hidden in the heart of the shattered city, guarded by the shadows of the past. Three keys will unlock its power, three sacrifices will awaken its wrath.'"

She looked up at Aric, her heart pounding. "This is it. This is what they're after."

Aric nodded, his expression grim. "Cindras Hold. The ruins of the city were abandoned after the Great War. It's a place of death and shadows. If the witches find the keys, they could unlock the *Lament* and unleash its power."

Elara felt a chill run down her spine. "We have to find it first."

"Yes," Aric agreed. "But first, we need to find those keys. And we need to figure out what kind of sacrifices they're talking about."

Elara nodded, determination hardening her resolve. They were on the brink of something terrible, something that could change the course of history. But she wasn't going to let fear stop her. Not now.

They gathered their things and made their way back out of the monastery, the shadows deepening around them as night fell. Elara glanced at Aric, his silhouette outlined against the faint glow of the moon. Whatever came next, they would face it together.

As they left the ruins behind, a figure watched them from the shadows, eyes glinting with malice and anticipation. The witches were not far behind, and the hunt had only just begun

Chapter 6: The Hidden Library

The journey to the hidden library was perilous and fraught with danger. The Guardians of the Flame, a reclusive order sworn to protect the ancient knowledge of the Fire Hunters, were known for their distrust of outsiders, even those who shared their cause. The library was said to be hidden deep within the Forbidden Peaks, surrounded by treacherous cliffs and shrouded in perpetual mist.

Aric and Elara made their way cautiously through the narrow mountain paths, the wind howling like a chorus of spirits around them. The air was thin and cold, and the sky above was a dark canopy of swirling clouds. It felt as though the very land itself was warning them away.

"Are you sure this is the right way?" Elara asked, her voice barely audible over the wind.

Aric nodded, his eyes scanning the rugged terrain. "It has to be. The map Elder Orin gave us is old, but it matches the landmarks we've seen. The library should be close by"

They pressed on, their movements slow and deliberate. Every step felt like a battle against the elements, and the path grew narrower and more treacherous as they ascended. Finally, after what felt like hours of climbing, they reached a narrow ledge that ended at a sheer rock face. Aric paused, examining the stone closely.

"There should be an entrance here," he murmured, running his fingers over the rough surface.

Elara watched as he traced the outline of a symbol etched into the rock—a flame enclosed within a circle. She felt a faint pulse of magic as Aric pressed his hand against the symbol and whispered an incantation in the old tongue of the Fire Hunters. The rock trembled, and then, with a low rumble, a section of the cliff slid away, revealing a narrow passageway.

Aric turned to her with a small, triumphant smile. "Found it."

They entered the passage, the air inside damp and heavy with the scent of old stone and earth. The walls were lined with runes that glowed faintly as they walked, lighting their way through the winding corridor. After several minutes, they emerged into a vast chamber filled with shelves upon shelves of books, scrolls, and artifacts. The library stretched as far as the eye could see, its high ceilings supported by massive stone pillars carved with intricate patterns.

Elara stared in awe. "This place is incredible."

"It's one of the oldest repositories of knowledge in the world," Aric said quietly. "The Guardians of the Flame have kept it hidden for centuries, protecting its secrets from those who would misuse them."

A figure stepped out from behind a pillar, cloaked in dark robes. His eyes, sharp and piercing, studied them with a mixture of curiosity and suspicion. "You should not be here."

Aric stepped forward, bowing his head slightly in respect. "We come in peace, Keeper. We seek knowledge that could help us stop the witches from unlocking the *Lament of Cindras*."

The Keeper's gaze shifted to Elara, and she felt the weight of his scrutiny. "You bring a witch among us?" he asked, his voice filled with a mixture of disdain and wariness.

"I'm not a witch," Elara said, meeting his gaze steadily. "But I need to understand what I am. And if there's something here that can help us stop the coven, we have to find it."

The Keeper studied her for a moment longer, then nodded slowly. "Very well. But know this: knowledge is a double-edged sword. It can grant you power, but it can also destroy you."

He gestured for them to follow and led them through the maze of shelves to a secluded section at the back of the library. The air here felt heavier, charged with the weight of ancient spells and forbidden lore. The Keeper stopped before a large, iron-bound tome, its cover marked with the same symbol they had seen on the rock outside.

"This is the Codex of Cindras," he said, his voice reverent. "It contains the history of the city and the secrets of the *Lament*."

Aric reached out to open the book, but the Keeper placed a hand on his arm, stopping him. "Before you read, you must understand. The *Lament of Cindras* was created in the darkest days of the Great War, forged from the despair and agony of those who perished. It is not just a weapon; it is a curse."

Elara felt a shiver run down her spine. "What do you mean?"

The Keeper's eyes were solemn. "The *Lament* has the power to tear open the veil between worlds, to unleash the spirits of the dead and the shadows that dwell in the void. But to wield such power requires great sacrifice. The keys to unlocking it are not just physical objects; they are bound to the souls of those who created it. To awaken the *Lament* fully, the coven will need more than just the keys—they will need to perform a ritual of blood and death."

Aric's expression hardened. "We have to find the keys before they do. Where are they?"

The Keeper opened the Codex, revealing a map of the ancient city of Cindras Hold. Three locations were marked with symbols: the Vault of Shadows, the Sanctuary of the Lost, and the Citadel of Ashes.

"The keys are hidden in these places," the Keeper said. "Each is protected by powerful wards and guardians that only those of great strength and will can overcome. But be warned—retrieving them will not be easy."

"We have to try," Elara said, determination burning in her eyes. "We can't let them get the keys. We can't let them use the *Lament*."

The Keeper nodded, his expression grave. "Then may the flames guide you. But remember, the path you walk is fraught with peril. Many have tried to unlock the secrets of the *Lament*, and all have failed. Do not underestimate its power, or the darkness that seeks to claim it."

Aric and Elara exchanged a glance, a silent promise passing between them. They had faced danger before, but this was different. This was a battle for the very soul of the world.

As they left the hidden library, the Keeper's warning echoed in their minds. They knew now where they needed to go, but the road ahead was shrouded in uncertainty and shadow. The stakes had never been higher, and the clock was ticking.

Chapter 7: Secrets of the Abyss

Elara stared into the depths of the Abyss, a swirling mass of shadows and whispers that seemed to call to her. The air was thick with an unnatural chill, and the echoes of their footsteps reverberated through the cavern like distant warnings.

"We can't turn back now," Aric said, glancing at her, determination etched on his face. "We've come too far."

She nodded, steeling herself. "Right. We need to find out what's down there."

As they descended deeper into the cavern, the light from their torches flickered against the stone walls, revealing ancient carvings that seemed to pulse with a life of their own. The symbols depicted battles between light and darkness, moments of triumph overshadowed by despair.

"What do you think it all means?" Mira asked, tracing her fingers along the carvings.

"It's history," Elara replied, her voice steady. "A record of the struggles against the darkness. We need to understand it if we're going to face whatever lies ahead."

Suddenly, a gust of wind swept through the cavern, extinguishing their torches and plunging them into darkness. Elara's heart raced as she fumbled for her magic. "Stay close!" she shouted, igniting a small flame in her palm.

The flickering light revealed the shadows coiling around them, shifting and whispering. "They're here," she breathed, fear creeping into her thoughts.

"Focus, Elara," Aric said, stepping closer. "We've faced darkness before. We can do it again."

With a deep breath, she pushed the fear away, channeling her magic into the flame. The light grew brighter, illuminating the cavern walls and revealing more symbols—warnings about the dangers that awaited them.

As they pressed forward, Elara's gaze was drawn to a large mural at the cavern's heart. It depicted a great battle where figures of light clashed against monstrous shadows, and at the center stood a figure cloaked in dark flames—the Harbinger.

"Who is she?" Mira asked, her voice trembling as they approached.

Elara studied the mural, her heart sinking. "She's a manifestation of the darkness, a force that feeds on fear and despair. We must be careful."

Suddenly, the shadows surged forward, as if drawn to their presence. Elara felt the energy in the air shift, a palpable tension building around them.

"They're reacting to us," Aric said, readying his sword. "We need to fight them off!"

"Wait!" Elara shouted, raising her hand. "There's something here… a connection."

As she focused, she could feel the remnants of magic flowing through the air—an ancient power still lingering in the cavern. "If we can harness this energy, it might help us."

Aric nodded, determination flickering in his eyes. "Then let's do it. We'll channel the light and push back the shadows."

Together, they formed a circle, hands joined as Elara concentrated on the energy surrounding them. She could feel the warmth of their combined strength, a surge of magic flowing through her.

"On my count," she said, taking a deep breath. "One… two… three!"

With a shout, they unleashed their power, sending waves of light cascading into the shadows. The darkness recoiled, shrieking as the light pushed through, illuminating the cavern once more.

But as the shadows retreated, the Harbinger's presence lingered, her laughter echoing in the depths. "You think you can defeat me?" she taunted, the words dripping with malice. "I am everywhere, in every fear you hold."

Elara gritted her teeth, fury igniting within her. "We will face you! You won't take our home!"

With the darkness momentarily at bay, Elara turned back to her companions. "We need to find a way to seal this place. If we don't, the shadows will continue to threaten us."

"Agreed," Aric replied, resolve shining in his eyes. "We'll figure it out together."

As they prepared to explore deeper into the cavern, the flicker of hope returned. They had faced the darkness and pushed it back for now, but the true battle was still ahead. Together, they would uncover the secrets of the Abyss and find a way to bring an end to the Harbinger's reign of terror once and for all.

Chapter 8: The Vault of Shadows

The flames flickered in the dark, casting elongated shadows that danced along the walls of the Vault. Elara felt the heat of her fire magic invigorate her, giving her strength as they pressed deeper into the ancient chamber. Aric fought beside her, his sword slicing through the darkness, each swing pushing the wraith-like spirits back.

"Focus on the key," he urged, dodging a shadow that lunged toward him. "We can't let them distract us!"

Elara nodded, her heart pounding as she scanned the cavernous space. The air crackled with energy, and she could feel the wards protecting the key pulsing like a heartbeat. They had to reach it before the spirits overwhelmed them.

As they moved further in, they spotted an ornate pedestal in the center of the chamber. Upon it rested a small, shimmering object that radiated a soft blue light—the first key. It was a beautiful, intricate piece, shaped like a flame, with runes etched into its surface.

"There it is!" Elara shouted, her eyes wide with determination.

But as they approached, the spirits surged forward, their forms twisting in rage. The air grew heavier, and a chorus of anguished cries echoed around them. "You shall not take it! This is our prison!"

Aric moved to shield Elara, swinging his sword to keep the spirits at bay. "We have to be quick! Grab the key!"

Elara summoned her magic again, the fire blazing brighter as she pushed against the dark tide. She felt a connection to the key, a pull that urged her closer. "On three! One… two…"

Before she could finish counting, she darted forward, extending her hand toward the key. As her fingers brushed its surface, a shockwave of energy surged through her, and she was suddenly surrounded by visions—flashes of the Great War, of sacrifices made, and of the *Lament* itself unleashing chaos.

"Grab it!" Aric shouted, and in that moment of hesitation, the shadows pressed in, their cold grasp threatening to drag her under.

With a fierce determination, Elara yanked the key free from the pedestal. The moment she did, a blinding light erupted from it, pushing the spirits back, shrieking in fury. The light enveloped her and Aric, shielding them from the shadows' grasp.

"Run!" Aric yelled, his voice cutting through the chaos.

They turned and sprinted back toward the entrance of the vault, the key glowing brightly in Elara's hand. The spirits wailed behind them, their forms distorting and twisting in the light. The ground trembled, and the very walls of the vault seemed to shudder in response to the power they had unleashed.

As they reached the archway, the shadows coalesced into a massive figure—a guardian of the vault, its form shifting between smoke and solid stone, its eyes glowing like embers. "You cannot leave!" it roared, the sound reverberating through the chamber.

Elara felt a surge of fear but steeled herself. "We have what we came for!" she shouted defiantly, holding the key aloft. "We'll fight if we have to!"

The guardian advanced, but before it could strike, Aric stepped forward, his sword raised high. "Together, Elara!"

With a swift motion, he slashed at the guardian, his blade igniting with a brilliant fire. Elara joined him, channeling her magic into the attack. Flames enveloped the guardian, momentarily illuminating the chamber with their brilliance.

"Now!" Aric shouted as they pushed forward, breaking through the guardian's defenses. They burst through the archway just as the chamber began to collapse behind them, dust and debris raining down around them.

They stumbled out into the cold night air, gasping for breath, and turned to see the vault sealed behind them, the entrance disappearing into solid rock. Elara felt a wave of relief wash over her, mingled with exhilaration. They had escaped, but the danger was far from over.

"Did we really just do that?" she panted, looking at the key in her hand, still shimmering faintly.

Aric glanced at her, a mixture of pride and disbelief on his face. "We did. But we need to move. The witches will know we have the key."

They set off into the dark, the weight of their mission pressing down on them like a storm cloud. As they navigated the ruins of Cindras Hold, they could feel the tension in the air. The echoes of the past lingered around them, and the shadows seemed to stretch longer with every step.

Chapter 9: Shadows of the Past

With the key safely in her possession, Elara felt a mixture of triumph and dread. They were one step closer to stopping the witches, but the reality of their situation hung over them like a dark cloud. They needed to find the next key, but the dangers of Cindras Hold were far from over.

"Where do we go next?" Elara asked, glancing at the map they had taken from the Codex. The second key was located in the Sanctuary of the Lost, marked by a symbol resembling a shattered mirror.

Aric studied the map, tracing the path with his finger. "It's not far from here. Just past the northern gate of the city. But we'll have to be careful. If the witches are searching for the keys, they'll be here soon."

As they navigated through the ruins, Elara couldn't shake the feeling that they were being watched. Shadows flickered at the edge of her vision, and every whisper of wind felt like a warning. She kept her magic close, ready to defend herself at a moment's notice.

They approached the northern gate, the remnants of ancient towers looming overhead. The air was thick with tension, and the shadows seemed to gather more densely around them. Elara felt a chill run down her spine, her instincts screaming that they were not alone.

Suddenly, a figure stepped out from the shadows—a woman clad in dark robes, her hair cascading like a waterfall of night. The air crackled with dark energy around her, and Elara's heart raced as she recognized the witch from the grove.

"Welcome to Cindras Hold, Fire Hunters," the witch said, her voice smooth and mocking. "I've been waiting for you."

"Why are you here?" Aric demanded, stepping protectively in front of Elara. "You won't stop us."

"Oh, but I already have," the witch replied, her lips curling into a sinister smile. "You've unwittingly done my work for me. The shadows are hungry, and they're eager to claim you."

With a flick of her wrist, the shadows around her writhed and twisted, taking shape as dark tendrils that lunged toward them. Elara felt a surge of fear, but she quickly focused, summoning her fire magic in response.

"Together!" she shouted, igniting a blaze that surged toward the shadows.

The fire met the darkness, illuminating the night in a fierce display of light and shadow. But the witch only laughed, her eyes glinting with amusement. "You think your flames can extinguish the shadows? They were born from darkness!"

Aric lunged forward, aiming for the witch, but she danced aside with unnatural grace, her laughter echoing in the air. "You're too late! The others are already searching for the final key. Soon, this city will belong to us!"

Elara felt a rush of determination surge through her. "We won't let that happen!"

With a roar, she unleashed a wave of fire, pushing the shadows back. Aric charged forward, striking at the witch with his sword. The clash of fire and dark magic crackled in the air, creating an electric tension that threatened to erupt.

But the witch was quick, and she danced just out of reach, her laughter a chilling reminder of the stakes at play. "You can't stop the inevitable!"

Elara could feel the weight of the shadows pressing down, but she refused to back down. "We will stop you!"

As the battle raged, she focused on her magic, channeling it deeper, feeling the fire within her roar to life. She had to find a way to break through the witch's defenses. In that moment, she remembered the stories of her ancestors, the legends of the Fire Hunters who had faced the darkness before.

"Aric, we need to combine our magic!" she called out, determination lighting her eyes.

He nodded, understanding what she meant. They had to join their powers if they wanted to overcome this darkness. "On my signal!"

They gathered their energy, the air around them crackling with tension. The witch sneered, sensing their intent but too late to react. "Fools!"

"Now!" Aric shouted.

In perfect synchrony, Elara unleashed her flames while Aric charged with his sword, merging their energies into a brilliant wave of light and heat. The fire surged forward, enveloping the witch and the shadows in a brilliant blaze. For a moment, the darkness recoiled, and Elara felt the weight of the shadows lift.

But the witch cackled, summoning the darkness back. "You think you've won? This is just the beginning!"

With a final surge of strength, Elara pushed her magic further, fueling the flames with every ounce of will she had. The shadows writhed, caught between the fire and the witch's control, but slowly, they began to falter.

"Now!" Aric shouted again.

Together, they pushed through, the combined force breaking through the witch's defenses. The flames consumed the darkness, and with a final, desperate scream, the witch was engulfed in the light, dissipating into the air like smoke.

As the fire subsided, Elara and Aric stood panting, the weight of the battle hanging heavily on their shoulders. The shadows that had surrounded them faded, leaving the night still and silent once more.

"Did we...?" Elara started, uncertainty creeping into her voice.

"We did," Aric replied, a mix of disbelief and relief washing over him. "But we need to move. The Sanctuary is still ahead, and we can't let our guard down."

They pressed on, the sense of victory mingled with the reality of what lay ahead. They had faced the witch and survived, but the hunt was far from over. The next key awaited them, and they had to be ready for whatever darkness awaited in the Sanctuary of the Lost.

Chapter 10: The Sanctuary of the Lost

Elara and Aric navigated the twisted streets of Cindras Hold, the shadows of the city still heavy in the air. The weight of their recent victory over the witch pulsed in Elara's veins, but a sense of urgency spurred them onward. They had to reach the Sanctuary of the Lost and retrieve the second key before the witches could close in.

As they approached the sanctuary, the architecture shifted dramatically. Where the vault had been a labyrinth of dark stone, the sanctuary stood tall and solemn, adorned with intricate carvings of celestial bodies and ancient heroes. Vines twisted up its walls, almost as if nature itself was attempting to reclaim what had been lost.

"Here it is," Aric murmured, gazing up at the grand entrance. The doors were massive, made of ancient wood, and etched with protective symbols. Elara felt a faint pulse of magic emanating from them.

Elara reached for the door, feeling a familiar warmth from the first key. "This feels right," she said, pushing against the heavy wood. To her surprise, the door swung open easily, revealing a vast hall bathed in soft, ethereal light.

Inside, the sanctuary was a stark contrast to the dark exterior. Golden light filtered through high, cracked windows, illuminating a collection of artifacts, relics, and remnants of the past. Elara felt a deep sense of reverence; this place held history, the echoes of those who had come before them.

"Stay alert," Aric warned, his eyes scanning the room. "This place is likely protected."

They moved cautiously through the hall, examining the relics. Each piece seemed to tell a story, whispering secrets of bravery and sacrifice. But the atmosphere was thick with tension, and Elara sensed they were not alone.

"Look," she pointed toward a raised platform at the end of the hall. A faint glow emanated from a pedestal in the center, similar to the one in the Vault of Shadows. "That must be it!"

As they approached the pedestal, the air around them shimmered, and a voice echoed through the sanctuary. "Who dares enter the Sanctuary of the Lost?"

Elara froze, her heart racing. A spectral figure materialized before them, clad in armor that gleamed like the stars. The spirit's eyes were filled with ancient wisdom and sadness. "You seek the key, but are you worthy?"

"We are the Fire Hunters," Aric declared, standing tall. "We seek to stop the witches from unleashing the *Lament of Cindras*."

"The *Lament*," the spirit murmured, a look of sorrow crossing its ethereal face. "A powerful curse, born from despair. To claim the key, you must prove your intentions. You must face the trials of the lost."

"What kind of trials?" Elara asked, her resolve unwavering.

"Trials of heart, mind, and spirit," the spirit replied. "You must confront your deepest fears and desires. Only then will you be deemed worthy to wield the key."

With a determined nod, Elara stepped forward. "We're ready."

The spirit raised a hand, and the sanctuary began to shift. The walls blurred, colors swirling around them until they found themselves in a darkened landscape, the ground shrouded in mist. The atmosphere was oppressive, thick with uncertainty and fear.

"Welcome to the Trial of the Lost," the spirit's voice echoed, though it seemed to come from all directions. "Face your truths, and only then may you pass."

Chapter 11: The Trials

The mists swirled around Elara and Aric, obscuring their surroundings. Elara's heart raced as she glanced at Aric, who looked equally tense. "What do you think will happen?" she whispered.

"I don't know, but we have to stick together," he replied, his voice steady despite the uncertainty.

Suddenly, the mist began to clear, revealing a dark forest filled with twisted trees and haunting echoes. Shadows flitted between the trunks, and an eerie silence enveloped them. Elara's pulse quickened, and she instinctively reached for her fire magic.

"Stay close," Aric urged, and they ventured deeper into the forest.

As they walked, a chilling wind swept through the trees, carrying whispers that clawed at Elara's mind. They spoke of doubts, failures, and fears she had tried to bury. The air felt heavy, each breath filled with a sense of impending doom.

"Do you hear that?" Elara asked, her voice trembling.

"It's just the trial," Aric said, but uncertainty flickered in his eyes. "Stay focused."

The shadows grew thicker, and suddenly, they were confronted by an apparition—Elara's mother, standing before her, bathed in an ethereal glow. Her expression was one of disappointment.

"Elara, why have you chosen this path?" her mother asked, her voice echoing with sorrow. "You were meant for greatness, but you walk into darkness."

Elara's heart ached at the sight. "I'm trying to protect our world, to understand my powers!"

"Your powers could destroy you, Elara. You must turn back before it's too late," the apparition warned, her voice laced with concern.

"No!" Elara shouted, pushing back against the wave of doubt that threatened to overwhelm her. "I can't turn back. I need to face this."

As the apparition faded, the forest shifted again, revealing Aric standing alone, surrounded by darkness. Shadows loomed over him, whispering his fears—the fear of failure, of losing Elara, of never being enough.

"Aric!" Elara cried, reaching out to him. The shadows pressed closer, and she could see the anguish on his face.

"Stay back, Elara! You don't understand!" he shouted, struggling against the darkness. "I can't protect you!"

"You're stronger than you think!" Elara shouted, her voice cutting through the shadows. "We're in this together!"

The shadows recoiled as Elara summoned her fire magic, illuminating the forest with a brilliant blaze. The darkness faded, revealing Aric, who looked at her with a mixture of relief and admiration.

"Thank you," he breathed, and together they stood against the remnants of their fears.

But the trial was far from over. The ground trembled beneath them, and the mist swirled again, pulling them into another realm—a vast, desolate battlefield where echoes of the past roared like a tempest.

Ghostly figures moved through the haze, trapped in an endless cycle of fighting. Among them was a familiar face—Elara's father, lost in the chaos of war. The sight tore at her heart.

"Father!" she cried, but her voice was drowned out by the clamor of battle.

"Stop!" Aric shouted, his eyes wide with shock. "We can't change the past!"

"I can't lose him again!" Elara responded, desperation flooding her. She reached for her father, but the shadows of the battlefield pulled him away, leaving her grasping at air.

"You must let go," the spirit's voice echoed around them. "To face the future, you must accept the past."

"No! I refuse!" Elara screamed, anger igniting her fire magic.

As flames erupted from her hands, the battlefield trembled, the shadows recoiling from the heat. But the ghosts of the past were relentless, and Elara felt herself being pulled into the memory of loss and despair.

"Fight it!" Aric urged, standing firm beside her. "Remember why you're here!"

With a fierce determination, Elara focused on her true purpose—the desire to protect those she loved, to understand her powers, and to stop the witches. The memories of her father's lessons, of the warmth of their shared moments, flooded her mind.

"I will not be defined by my fears!" she shouted, the fire roaring to life around her. "I will forge my own path!"

The battlefield shimmered, and slowly, the ghostly figures began to fade, releasing Elara from the grip of the past. She felt the weight lift, and the fire within her surged with newfound strength.

As the battlefield dissolved, the mist cleared once more, revealing the spirit from before. "You have faced your trials and confronted your truths," it proclaimed, its voice resonating with approval. "You have proven yourselves worthy."

The sanctuary around them reformed, and the pedestal gleamed before them, the second key resting atop it. Elara reached for it, her heart racing with excitement. As her fingers closed around the key, she felt a wave of power surge through her.

"You have claimed the second key," the spirit said. "But your journey is far from over. The final key lies within the Citadel of Ashes. Beware, for the witches will not rest until they have claimed what is rightfully theirs."

Elara and Aric exchanged a determined glance, the weight of their mission clear. They had faced their fears, emerged stronger, and now they had to confront the final challenge ahead. The witches were closing in, and they had to act quickly.

With the second key secured, they set their sights on the Citadel of Ashes, ready to face whatever darkness awaited them

Chapter 12: The Path to the Citadel

With the second key now in their possession, Elara and Aric stepped out of the Sanctuary of the Lost, the night air sharp against their skin. The stars above twinkled like shards of hope, but they both knew that danger lurked nearby.

"We need to move quickly," Aric said, glancing back at the sanctuary. "The witches won't take long to realize what we've done."

Elara nodded, feeling the weight of the keys hanging at her side—a tangible reminder of their mission. The path to the Citadel of Ashes lay to the south, beyond the ruins of the old city. The legends spoke of it as a place steeped in dark magic, where the witches conducted their rituals to summon the *Lament of Cindras*.

"Let's take the back roads," Elara suggested, remembering the narrow alleys that could help them avoid any witch patrols.

As they navigated the dimly lit streets, the atmosphere shifted. Shadows seemed to stretch and twist, forming dark shapes that lurked just beyond their sight. Elara tightened her grip on the second key, its warmth reassuring against the chill in the air.

"Do you think we'll really find the third key at the Citadel?" Aric asked, breaking the silence.

"I have to believe it," Elara replied, her determination hardening. "If we find it, we can stop the witches from unleashing the *Lament*. We can protect our home."

Their footsteps echoed softly as they slipped through the winding alleys, the ruins whispering secrets of a long-gone era. But as they approached the edge of the city, a sudden flicker of movement caught Elara's eye.

"Wait!" she hissed, raising a hand to stop Aric. They crouched behind a crumbling wall, peering out into the open space ahead.

A group of witches gathered near the entrance to the Citadel, their dark robes swirling like smoke in the wind. Elara recognized one of them—the same witch they had fought before, her eyes glinting with malice.

"They're waiting for us," Aric whispered, tension radiating off him.

"We can't confront them directly," Elara said, scanning the area. "There's got to be another way in."

"Look," Aric pointed toward a narrow path veering off to the left, obscured by thick underbrush. "We can take that route. It might lead us around."

"Let's do it," Elara agreed, and they slipped quietly into the shadows, moving with purpose. The thickets closed in around them, but Elara felt the strength of their resolve guiding them forward.

As they crept through the underbrush, the sounds of the witches faded behind them. Elara's heart pounded with adrenaline, a mixture of fear and anticipation coursing through her veins.

After what felt like an eternity, they emerged onto a small clearing. Before them stood the Citadel of Ashes, its towering spires looming against the night sky. The air around it shimmered with dark energy, and an uneasy feeling settled in Elara's stomach.

"Are you ready?" Aric asked, his expression serious.

"Ready as I'll ever be," Elara replied, steeling herself for what lay ahead. Together, they approached the massive doors of the citadel, their minds focused on the task at hand.

Chapter 13: Into the Ashes

The doors of the Citadel loomed before them, massive and foreboding. Elara felt a chill wash over her as she placed her hands against the cold wood, the ancient runes etched into its surface pulsing with dark energy.

"Let's see if this works," Aric said, positioning the second key into a slot beneath the door's intricate carvings. With a deep breath, he twisted the key, and the doors creaked open, revealing a dimly lit hall beyond.

As they stepped inside, the air thickened with an oppressive magic that made Elara's skin crawl. The citadel was a stark contrast to the sanctuary they had just left—where the sanctuary had been filled with light and hope, this place was steeped in shadow and despair.

"Stay close," Aric whispered, drawing his sword. Elara felt her fire magic simmering just below the surface, ready to ignite at a moment's notice.

They moved cautiously through the hall, lined with faded tapestries depicting battles and dark rituals. Elara could feel the weight of the history surrounding them, the echoes of lost souls trapped within these walls.

Suddenly, a flicker of movement caught her eye. A figure emerged from the shadows—a woman with wild hair and piercing eyes, her presence radiating power. Elara recognized her instantly: the witch who had taunted them outside the sanctuary.

"Welcome to the Citadel of Ashes, Fire Hunters," the witch said, her voice dripping with disdain. "You've come far, but your journey ends here."

"What do you want?" Aric demanded, stepping protectively in front of Elara.

"To protect what is mine," the witch replied, her eyes glinting with malice. "You are foolish to think you can wield the keys against us. The *Lament* will be unleashed, and you will not survive the night."

Elara felt a surge of anger and defiance. "We will stop you! You won't get the chance to complete your ritual!"

The witch laughed, a cold, echoing sound that sent chills down Elara's spine. "You think you can challenge me? You are but children playing with fire."

With a flick of her wrist, shadows erupted around her, twisting into dark tendrils that lunged toward Elara and Aric.

"Together!" Aric shouted, raising his sword.

Elara summoned her fire magic, the flames erupting from her hands in a brilliant blaze. The two powers collided with the shadows, illuminating the hall and creating a shockwave that sent the tendrils reeling back.

"Keep pushing!" Elara yelled, feeling the fire within her roar to life. They surged forward, determined to confront the witch and protect the keys.

But the witch was quick, dodging their attacks with an agility that belied her dark nature. "You cannot defeat me! I am the mistress of shadows!"

As Elara and Aric pressed on, they felt the weight of the citadel pressing down on them, the dark magic swirling like a storm. Shadows danced around them, forming shapes that whispered doubts and fears, but Elara pushed back, drawing strength from her fire and the bond she shared with Aric.

"Don't listen to her!" Aric shouted, deflecting a shadow with his sword. "We're stronger together!"

With renewed determination, Elara focused her energy into a massive burst of flames, aiming directly at the witch. "You will not win!"

The flames surged forward, illuminating the darkness, and for a brief moment, Elara saw the witch's expression shift from confidence to surprise. But in that instant, shadows swirled around her, absorbing the flames and reflecting them back in a furious wave.

"Foolish children," the witch sneered, her voice resonating with power. "You think you can stop the inevitable?"

As the shadows closed in, Elara felt a flicker of doubt creep into her heart. But then she remembered the faces of her loved ones, the people she was fighting for. She couldn't let the darkness consume them.

"Aric!" she called, and he met her gaze, understanding the unspoken bond between them. They needed to combine their magic once more.

"Now!" Aric yelled, and they unleashed their powers in perfect harmony—a blazing inferno infused with the light of hope.

The resulting explosion of light shattered the shadows, illuminating the citadel and pushing the witch back. For a moment, Elara felt invincible, the darkness retreating before their combined strength.

But the witch was not defeated yet. With a furious snarl, she summoned the darkness back, her eyes glowing with rage. "You will pay for this!"

Elara and Aric braced themselves, ready to face whatever came next. They had fought hard to reach this point, and they would not back down now. The final key awaited them, and they would do whatever it took to stop the witches from unleashing the *Lament of Cindras*

Chapter 14: The Heart of Darkness

The witch staggered but quickly regained her footing, her eyes narrowing as she surveyed Elara and Aric with a newfound fury. The shadows around her thickened, coiling like serpents ready to strike.

"You think you can defeat me with mere flames?" she taunted, her voice laced with venom. "I am the embodiment of darkness itself!"

Elara felt the heat of her fire magic surge again, but she knew they needed a different strategy. "Aric, we can't fight her alone! We need to find a way to weaken her connection to this place."

"Right!" Aric agreed, looking around frantically for something they could use. "There must be something here!"

As they scanned the citadel's vast hall, Elara remembered the tapestries that lined the walls. "Those might hold the key to understanding her power," she said, pointing to a mural depicting the citadel's founding.

With a nod, they dashed toward the nearest tapestry, the air crackling with tension as the witch advanced. Elara reached out, her fingers brushing the ancient fabric, feeling a pulse of energy course through her.

The tapestry showed a battle—figures of warriors and witches clashing amidst swirling flames and shadows. But at the center, a glowing crystal was depicted, pulsing with light, illuminating the scene. Elara's heart raced; that must be the source of the citadel's dark power.

"Aric! Look!" she shouted, her eyes wide. "That crystal! If we can reach it, we might be able to disrupt her magic!"

"Then we need to make a distraction," he said, determination hardening his voice.

Elara nodded, her mind racing. "I'll hold her off. You go for the crystal!"

"Are you sure?" Aric's brow furrowed with concern.

"Just trust me! I'll be right behind you," Elara insisted.

With a shared look of resolve, they split up. Elara faced the witch, igniting her magic. "You won't take this place from us!"

The witch sneered, summoning shadows that lunged toward Elara. She unleashed a torrent of flames, illuminating the hall and pushing back the encroaching darkness. The two powers clashed, creating a spectacle of light and shadow.

"Foolish girl!" the witch shouted, her voice rising above the chaos. "You think you can protect what is not yours?"

As Elara fought, she felt the shadows closing in again, but she held her ground, her fire blazing bright. Meanwhile, Aric made his way toward the pedestal, the crystal glowing in the dim light.

"Almost there!" he muttered, dodging tendrils of shadow that reached out to ensnare him.

"Keep going!" Elara yelled, summoning all her energy into a concentrated flame, pushing against the witch's dark magic.

Aric finally reached the pedestal, breathless and focused. The crystal pulsed with energy, and he could feel its warmth. He grasped it tightly, and for a moment, everything fell silent.

Chapter 15: The Shattering

As Aric held the crystal, a surge of power flooded through him, connecting him to the citadel's ancient magic. Images flashed before his eyes—past battles, lost souls, and the dark rituals that had taken place within these walls. He understood now that the crystal was the heart of the citadel, a source of both power and vulnerability.

"Now, Elara!" he shouted, his voice filled with urgency.

With a deep breath, Aric channeled the crystal's energy, focusing it on the witch who had turned to face him, her expression a mixture of confusion and anger.

"What are you doing?" she roared, her shadows lashing out wildly.

"I'm ending this!" Aric declared, unleashing a beam of radiant light from the crystal toward her. The light sliced through the darkness, illuminating the hall in a brilliant glow.

Elara, feeling the surge of energy, reinforced it with her fire magic. "Together!" she called out, and the combined power surged forward, engulfing the witch in a blinding explosion of light.

"No!" the witch screamed, her shadows dissolving into wisps of smoke as the light consumed her. The citadel trembled, the very foundation shaking as the dark magic began to unravel.

Elara felt a rush of relief but knew they needed to act fast. "The keys!" she shouted. "We have to use them together!"

Aric nodded, quickly joining her side as they held up the first and second keys. The radiant energy from the crystal fused with their magic, creating a swirling vortex of light that enveloped them.

With a deep breath, they pressed the keys against the ground, channeling their combined power into the very heart of the citadel. The keys pulsed with energy, and as they did, the shadows writhed in agony, the witch's magic collapsing under the onslaught.

"Now!" Elara cried, and they focused their energy, pushing the light deeper into the citadel's core.

The crystal shattered with a resounding crack, sending shards of radiant light spiraling through the air. The dark magic that had suffocated the citadel for so long began to break apart, releasing the lost souls trapped within.

As the light flooded the hall, Elara and Aric shielded their eyes. The shadows dissipated, and a feeling of warmth and peace washed over them. The citadel was transforming, its dark past purged, replaced by a vibrant energy that pulsed with life.

When the light dimmed, they stood amid the remnants of the citadel, now a sanctuary of hope. The witch was gone, her darkness erased. Elara felt a deep sense of accomplishment, but there was no time to celebrate yet.

"The final key," she whispered, glancing around the room. "It has to be here somewhere."

Aric nodded, his eyes scanning the area for any sign of the last key. "We've come too far to stop now."

As they searched, a soft glow caught Elara's attention, emanating from the far side of the hall. There, amidst the ruins, lay a pedestal—an empty space waiting for them.

"Over there!" Elara exclaimed, rushing toward the light.

As they approached, they felt the warmth of the final key, its presence calling to them like a beacon of hope. This was it—the culmination of their journey, the last piece in the puzzle that would allow them to confront the true threat of the witches.

With determination, Elara and Aric stepped forward, ready to claim the final key and face whatever lay ahead

Chapter 16: The Final Key

As Elara and Aric approached the pedestal, the warm glow intensified, illuminating their faces with a soft light. The air around them seemed to hum with anticipation, as if the very walls of the citadel recognized the significance of this moment.

"There it is," Aric said, his voice a mix of awe and excitement. "The final key."

Elara stepped forward, feeling a deep connection to the key even before she reached it. It rested upon the pedestal like a treasure, shaped like a flame, its surface etched with intricate symbols that pulsed in rhythm with her heartbeat.

"What if it's guarded?" Aric asked, his brow furrowing as he surveyed the area. "We need to be cautious."

Elara nodded, her senses heightened. "Let's be careful. We don't know what other defenses this place might have."

As Elara reached out, her fingers brushed the surface of the key. Instantly, a wave of energy surged through her, igniting her magic and flooding her with memories of her journey—the struggles, the fears, the victories. She felt the weight of the past and the hope of the future intertwine, fueling her resolve.

"Do you feel that?" Aric asked, stepping closer. "It's like it's alive."

"It is," Elara replied, her voice barely above a whisper. "This key holds the essence of our fight against the darkness."

Just as she lifted the key from the pedestal, a tremor shook the ground beneath them. The citadel groaned, remnants of its dark magic struggling against the light they had unleashed.

"We need to go!" Aric urged, his eyes wide with urgency.

Elara nodded, clutching the final key tightly in her hand. As they turned to flee, the shadows that had been vanquished began to stir again, swirling around them as if the very essence of the witch's power was trying to reclaim what it had lost.

"Quick!" Aric shouted, raising his sword. "We can't let them close in!"

Elara ignited her magic, flames erupting in a protective barrier around them. "Let's push through!"

They ran toward the exit, the shadows lunging forward with a renewed ferocity. Elara could feel their grasping tendrils trying to drag her back, but she refused to yield. With a fierce cry, she unleashed a torrent of fire, illuminating the darkness and forging a path ahead.

"Keep going!" Aric shouted, slashing at the shadows that sought to impede their escape.

They barreled through the crumbling halls of the citadel, the walls shaking with the struggle between light and dark. Just as they neared the entrance, a wave of shadows surged toward them, more powerful than before.

"Together!" Elara yelled, channeling her magic into a concentrated blast of flames.

Aric raised his sword high, echoing her call. "Together!"

With their powers combined, they unleashed a brilliant wave of light that shattered the encroaching darkness, propelling them forward. The entrance loomed ahead, and with one final push, they burst into the open air.

Chapter 17: The Gathering Storm

Outside, the night was starkly quiet. The stars twinkled overhead, a reminder of the vastness of the world beyond the citadel's dark embrace. Elara and Aric collapsed to the ground, panting, their hearts racing from the adrenaline of their escape.

"We made it," Aric gasped, relief flooding his voice.

Elara held the final key tightly, its warmth grounding her amidst the chaos of emotions. "But it's not over yet. We have the keys, but we still need to confront the witches and stop the *Lament of Cindras*."

"Right," Aric said, glancing back at the citadel. "The darkness is still out there. We need to move before they regroup."

Elara nodded, feeling the weight of their mission. "We head to the Valley of Whispers. That's where the witches are gathering for the ritual."

The journey to the valley was fraught with tension, every rustle in the night air setting Elara's senses on high alert. They navigated through the thick forest, the moonlight guiding their path, but a sense of foreboding clung to them like a shadow.

"We should be close," Aric said, squinting into the darkness ahead. "The valley should be just beyond this ridge."

As they crested the hill, the valley unfolded before them—a vast expanse bathed in silver moonlight. At its center stood an ancient stone altar, the ground around it marked with strange symbols. A group of witches encircled the altar, their dark robes billowing like storm clouds as they prepared for the ritual.

"There they are," Elara whispered, her heart pounding.

"Do we wait for the right moment?" Aric suggested, his grip tightening around his sword.

"No," Elara replied, a surge of determination rising within her. "We have the keys. We can't wait for them to complete the ritual. We have to disrupt it now!"

"Are you sure?" he asked, concern flickering in his eyes.

"Yes," she insisted. "This is our chance to stop them before they can summon the *Lament*."

"Then let's do it," Aric said, resolute.

With a fierce cry, they charged down the hill, their combined magic igniting the night. The witches turned, their expressions shifting from focus to shock as the two Fire Hunters approached, keys in hand, ready to fight for their world.

"Stop them!" one of the witches shrieked, raising her arms as dark magic crackled in the air.

Elara felt the weight of the keys in her hands, their power coursing through her. "We won't let you unleash your darkness!" she shouted, igniting her flames.

As they reached the edge of the altar, Elara and Aric stood side by side, ready to confront the witches and face the darkness that threatened to engulf their world. The final battle was upon them, and they would fight to protect everything they held dear.

Chapter 18: The Clash of Flames and Shadows

The air crackled with tension as Elara and Aric stood before the witches, the final key pulsing with power in Elara's grasp. The witches gathered their dark energy, eyes narrowing with malevolence as they prepared to counter the Fire Hunters' charge.

"You dare to challenge us?" the lead witch sneered, her voice echoing ominously across the valley. "You will pay for your insolence!"

"Not if we can help it!" Elara shouted, raising the final key high. Its light flared, illuminating the valley in a warm glow that pushed back the shadows.

"Aric, on my count!" she urged, feeling the surge of energy flow between them.

"Ready when you are," he replied, determination etched on his face.

"Three… two… one… now!" Elara cried, unleashing a wave of fire that engulfed the nearest witches. The flames roared to life, creating a barrier of heat and light that seared through the dark magic surrounding them.

Aric charged alongside her, slashing through the chaos, his sword gleaming. "Keep pushing!" he urged, his voice strong amidst the cacophony.

The witches retaliated, dark tendrils of magic snapping toward them like striking snakes. But Elara was ready; she focused her energy, sending a concentrated blast of flames to intercept the shadows. The two forces collided with a thunderous roar, scattering embers and darkness alike.

"We have to reach the altar!" Elara shouted, feeling the power of the keys surge within her.

They maneuvered through the fray, dodging spells and shadows, their bond amplifying their magic. Elara could sense the fear in the witches as they saw their dark spells falter against their fiery onslaught.

"Split up!" Aric suggested, spotting a gap in the witches' formation. "We can flank them!"

Elara nodded, adrenaline pumping through her veins. They moved in perfect synchrony, Aric charging left while Elara veered right, each of them targeting the witches who were forming the dark circle around the altar.

As Elara approached, she could see the altar's intricate symbols glowing faintly, a sign that the ritual was still in progress. The lead witch, realizing the urgency of the situation, shouted incantations that filled the air with dark energy.

"Elara!" Aric called, dodging a wave of shadows. "We need to disrupt their chant!"

"On it!" Elara replied, gathering her fire magic. She focused on the lead witch, the one whose power radiated the strongest.

With a fierce cry, she unleashed a torrent of flames directly at the witch, who raised her hands to shield herself. The fire met an invisible barrier, but Elara pushed through, forcing the flames to expand and break the witch's concentration.

"Stop her!" the lead witch screamed, her voice a mix of fury and desperation.

But Elara felt the tides of battle shifting. The other witches were struggling to maintain their focus, the energy of the ritual faltering. She seized the opportunity and charged forward, her flames illuminating the darkness around her.

As she reached the altar, the symbols began to flicker, the energy of the ritual weakening. "Aric, now!" she yelled, summoning every ounce of magic within her.

Aric sprinted toward the altar, his sword raised high. "For our home!" he shouted, striking down at the ground beside the altar, channeling his energy into a powerful wave of light.

The combination of fire and light surged through the altar, igniting the symbols and pushing back the shadows that threatened to engulf them. The witches shrieked, their dark magic unraveling as the radiant energy enveloped them.

"No! This cannot be!" the lead witch cried, panic flooding her voice.

Elara focused on the final key, its warmth spreading through her, fueling her resolve. "You will not unleash the *Lament of Cindras*!" she declared, slamming the key into the altar's center.

The ground trembled beneath them, and a shockwave of light erupted from the altar, cascading through the valley. The witches stumbled, their dark robes disintegrating under the force of the magic. Shadows screeched in protest, swirling wildly as the energy continued to expand.

Aric stood beside Elara, his expression a mix of awe and determination. "We're almost there!" he shouted above the chaos.

Together, they pushed their magic into the altar, intertwining their flames and light with the ancient energy of the citadel. The altar responded, glowing fiercely as the dark ritual was dismantled piece by piece.

"Together!" Elara urged, their powers resonating with one another. "We can end this!"

With one final surge of combined strength, they unleashed a brilliant explosion of fire and light, engulfing the valley. The darkness shattered like glass, sending shards of shadow scattering into the night.

The lead witch screamed, her voice lost in the whirlwind of energy as the remnants of her dark magic were obliterated. The remaining witches were swept away, their forms dissolving into wisps of smoke.

As the light faded, the valley fell silent, the remnants of the battle replaced by an eerie stillness. Elara and Aric stood together, panting, the keys still glowing softly in their hands.

"We did it," Aric whispered, disbelief evident in his voice.

Elara glanced around, taking in the transformed landscape. The shadows that had once suffocated the valley were gone, replaced by a gentle glow of hope. "We stopped the *Lament*," she said, a smile breaking through her exhaustion.

But as they took a moment to breathe, a low rumble echoed from the depths of the valley. Elara's heart raced as she turned to Aric. "What was that?"

"I don't know," he replied, eyes widening. "But we might not be done yet."

In the aftermath of their victory, a new challenge loomed on the horizon, and the Fire Hunters were determined to face it together

Chapter 19: Echoes of the Past

The low rumble grew louder, reverberating through the valley and sending tremors through the ground beneath Elara and Aric's feet. Unease settled in Elara's stomach as she scanned their surroundings, the remnants of the battle still crackling in the air.

"What now?" Aric asked, his grip tightening on his sword.

"I'm not sure," Elara replied, her gaze fixed on the altar, which pulsed with a strange energy, remnants of their combined magic flickering like dying embers. "But we should investigate. There might be something we missed."

They cautiously approached the altar, the air thick with tension. As they drew nearer, the rumbling intensified, and the ground began to shake beneath them.

"Stand back!" Aric shouted, raising his sword defensively.

Elara took a step closer, drawn by an inexplicable force. "Wait! I think it's coming from the altar!"

Just as she spoke, the symbols on the altar began to glow fiercely, and with a violent crack, the stone split open, revealing a dark chasm beneath. A swirling vortex of energy pulsed from the depths, casting shadows that danced erratically across the valley.

"What is that?" Aric exclaimed, stepping back as the vortex widened.

"I don't know, but we need to be careful," Elara said, feeling a mix of fear and curiosity. "It could be the source of the witches' power."

From the depths of the chasm, a voice echoed, low and resonant, sending chills down their spines. "You dare disturb my slumber?"

Elara's heart raced as she strained to see into the darkness. "Who are you?" she called out, her voice steady despite the fear clawing at her insides.

"I am the Guardian of the Citadel," the voice boomed. "For centuries, I have been bound to this place, overseeing the balance of light and dark. You have disrupted my realm, and now the consequences shall unfold."

"Consequences?" Aric echoed, his brow furrowing. "What do you mean?"

The ground shook violently, and the vortex pulsed again, sending a wave of dark energy that knocked them off their feet. Elara struggled to regain her balance, her instincts screaming for her to run.

"You have unleashed powers beyond your comprehension," the Guardian warned. "The darkness is not merely gone; it has awakened. The *Lament of Cindras* was but a fragment of a greater force, one that seeks to reclaim its dominion over this world."

"What can we do?" Elara shouted, fear and determination mingling in her voice. "We defeated the witches! We stopped the ritual!"

"Defeating them was but a battle," the Guardian intoned, the shadows swirling in the chasm as if alive. "To win the war, you must confront the heart of the darkness."

"And where is that?" Aric asked, glancing at Elara.

"Within the depths of the citadel lies the source," the Guardian replied. "You must descend into the Abyss of Shadows, face the remnants of the witches' power, and seal it once more. Only then can balance be restored."

Elara exchanged a determined look with Aric. "We can do this," she said, steeling her resolve. "We've come too far to back down now."

The Guardian's voice softened, a note of approval threading through the ominous tone. "Your courage is commendable. But beware, for the shadows are cunning, and they will seek to manipulate your fears."

With a deep breath, Elara stepped forward, looking down into the swirling darkness. "Then we'll face them together. We won't let the darkness win."

As they prepared to descend, the Guardian spoke once more. "Take the keys with you. They will guide your path and protect you from the shadows that seek to ensnare your souls."

Elara nodded, clutching the keys tightly. They would be her light in the darkness ahead.

"Let's go," she said, determination hardening her voice. With Aric by her side, they stepped into the chasm, the darkness enveloping them as they descended into the Abyss of Shadows, ready to confront whatever lay waiting in the depths below.

Chapter 20: Into the Abyss

The descent felt endless, the air growing colder and heavier with each passing moment. As they plunged deeper into the chasm, the light from above faded, replaced by a creeping darkness that seemed to pulse with life.

Elara held the keys tightly, their warmth a comforting presence against the chill that surrounded them. "Stay close," she whispered to Aric, her heart racing with a mix of fear and anticipation.

As they reached the bottom, they emerged into a vast cavern illuminated by faint, flickering lights—will-o'-the-wisps danced along the walls, casting eerie shadows that shifted and swirled. The air hummed with dark energy, a palpable tension that made Elara's skin prickle.

"This place feels… wrong," Aric said, his voice low as he surveyed the cavern.

"I can feel it too," Elara replied, unease creeping into her heart. "But we have to keep moving. The heart of the darkness is close."

They stepped forward cautiously, the echoes of their footsteps blending with the whispers of the cavern. The walls were slick with moisture, glistening like obsidian, and every now and then, Elara caught a glimpse of shadows flitting just beyond the reach of the light.

"Look," Aric pointed to a series of ancient carvings etched into the walls. "These might tell us what we're up against."

Elara leaned closer, her fingers brushing over the intricate designs. They depicted scenes of battles between light and dark, the rise and fall of powerful figures. But one image stood out—a shadowy figure, cloaked and menacing, standing at the center of a swirling vortex.

"What is that?" she murmured, a sense of dread settling in her stomach.

"That could be the darkness we're facing," Aric said, his brow furrowed. "It looks powerful."

"We have to be ready for anything," Elara replied, her voice resolute. "If that figure represents the source of the witches' power, we need to confront it and seal it away."

As they continued deeper into the cavern, the whispers grew louder, swirling around them like a haunting melody. Elara could feel her fears creeping in, the shadows beckoning her to give in to despair.

"Stay strong," she urged herself, shaking her head to clear the doubts. She glanced at Aric, who met her gaze with unwavering determination. They would not let the darkness win.

Suddenly, a cold wind swept through the cavern, extinguishing the will-o'-the-wisps in an instant. The shadows surged, forming into twisted shapes that reached out for them.

"Look out!" Aric shouted, drawing his sword.

Elara raised her hands, summoning her fire magic. "We can't let them surround us!"

Flames erupted from her palms, illuminating the cavern as shadows recoiled in fear. "Keep moving!" she urged, her heart pounding.

They dashed through the encroaching darkness, pushing deeper into the heart of the cavern. The air crackled with energy, the shadows growing more agitated as they fought against the light.

As they neared the center of the cavern, a massive stone altar rose before them, the source of the swirling darkness they had felt since entering. Atop the altar lay a crystal, dark and ominous, pulsing with shadowy energy.

"There it is," Elara breathed, her heart racing. "That must be the heart of the darkness."

Aric's grip on his sword tightened. "We need to destroy it."

"Together," Elara affirmed, feeling the keys thrumming with energy in her hands. They had to act quickly before the shadows could regain their strength.

As they approached the altar, the shadows writhed around them, coiling like serpents, trying to ensnare their feet. Elara held her ground, channeling her magic into the keys, their light pushing back against the encroaching darkness.

"Now!" she shouted, raising the keys high as Aric charged forward.

They unleashed their combined magic, fire and light colliding with the dark crystal atop the altar. The resulting explosion sent shockwaves through the cavern, illuminating the darkness and shattering the silence.

The shadows screamed, their forms dissolving into wisps of smoke as the crystal cracked and splintered. Light surged forth, engulfing the cavern and pushing back the shadows that had tormented them.

Elara and Aric stood their ground, pouring their energy into the blast, determined to end the threat once and for all. They could feel the darkness faltering, the very fabric of its power unraveling.

But just as victory seemed within reach, a dark figure emerged from the depths, rising above the altar with a chilling presence. Its eyes glowed with malice, and a sinister smile spread across its face.

"You think you can defeat me?" it taunted, the shadows swirling around it like a cloak. "I am the darkness incarnate!"

Elara's heart sank. They had awakened something far more powerful than they had anticipated

Chapter 21: The Darkness Incarnate

The figure loomed over them, a terrifying amalgamation of shadows and dark energy, its eyes glimmering with an unsettling light. Elara felt her heart race, fear clawing at her as she faced the embodiment of all they had fought against.

"Stay together!" Aric shouted, his voice steady despite the chill in the air. "We can't let it divide us!"

Elara nodded, clenching the keys in her hands. "We've faced darkness before. We can do this."

The dark figure laughed, a sound like shattering glass. "Foolish mortals! Your flames and light are nothing compared to the abyss within me. You think you can defeat what you cannot even comprehend?"

With a wave of its hand, the shadows surged forward, a tidal wave of darkness crashing toward them. Elara reacted instinctively, unleashing a wall of fire that pushed against the oncoming shadows. The heat clashed with the cold, creating a whirlwind of energy that illuminated the cavern.

"Aric, we need to find a way to weaken it!" Elara shouted, her focus split between maintaining the barrier and searching for an opening.

Aric nodded, darting to the side to flank the darkness. "I'll draw its attention! You focus on the keys!"

The shadows writhed as Aric charged forward, sword raised high. "You want a fight? Come and get me!" he yelled, his voice echoing defiantly.

Elara watched as Aric's bravery ignited something within her. She raised the keys, feeling their warmth surging through her veins. "I can do this," she whispered, recalling the strength of her magic.

As Aric engaged the dark figure, Elara began to chant an incantation, drawing upon the ancient magic of the keys. The symbols carved into them glowed with a radiant light, pulsing in time with her heartbeat.

"Key of Fire, ignite the shadows! Key of Light, banish the dark!" she cried, her voice rising in fervor. The keys resonated with her words, sending beams of light cascading toward the dark figure.

The creature turned, its expression shifting from amusement to anger as the light struck it. "No! You cannot—" it roared, the shadows around it twisting violently.

Seizing the moment, Aric launched himself forward, his sword gleaming in the flickering light. He struck at the heart of the darkness, hoping to pierce through its defenses.

But the dark figure retaliated, raising its hand to deflect Aric's blow. "You think your weapons can harm me?" it sneered, darkness coiling around its form like a serpent.

Elara felt a surge of panic, but she pushed it down. "Aric, keep fighting!" she urged, channeling more energy into the keys.

"Hold on!" he called back, his determination unwavering. He struck again, trying to find a weakness, a crack in the darkness.

Elara focused on the keys, their magic intertwining with her own. "Together, we can do this!" she shouted, feeling the power building within her.

The dark figure laughed again, this time more menacing. "Your unity will not save you from your own fears!"

With a wave of its hand, the shadows surged again, twisting into nightmarish forms that reflected Elara's deepest insecurities—visions of failure, loss, and despair flooded her mind. She staggered back, momentarily overwhelmed.

"Elara!" Aric shouted, slicing through the shadows to reach her. "Fight it! Remember why we're here!"

He was right. She couldn't let the darkness win. With a deep breath, she pushed the visions away, focusing on the warmth of the keys and the strength of their bond.

"Key of Fire, Key of Light!" Elara chanted again, her voice stronger. "Together, we shall prevail!"

The keys blazed with renewed intensity, casting a brilliant light that pushed back the shadows. The dark figure faltered, its form wavering as the magic encroached upon it.

"Enough!" it bellowed, summoning a storm of shadows that rushed toward them.

"Aric, now!" Elara cried, channeling all her energy into the keys.

As the darkness approached, Aric positioned himself protectively in front of Elara, sword raised. "We're not afraid of you!" he shouted, his voice cutting through the fear.

With a final incantation, Elara thrust the keys forward, unleashing a torrent of fire and light that surged toward the dark figure. The energy collided with the shadows, creating a blinding explosion that lit up the entire cavern.

"NO!" the figure shrieked, its form disintegrating under the overwhelming force.

The shadows twisted and writhed, but the light consumed them, banishing the darkness with a final, deafening roar. The cavern shook, and Elara could feel the very foundations of the Abyss shifting as the heart of the darkness began to crumble.

"Keep pushing!" Aric urged, determination etched into every feature.

Elara poured everything she had into the blast, the keys glowing brighter than ever before. The light expanded, enveloping the dark figure entirely, until with a final surge, it shattered into a thousand fragments, scattering into the ether.

The cavern fell silent, the remnants of the shadows dissipating into nothingness. Elara and Aric stood side by side, panting heavily, the glow of the keys dimming but still warm in their hands.

"We did it," Aric breathed, disbelief mingling with relief.

Elara looked around, taking in the transformed cavern. The oppressive darkness was gone, replaced by a soft, warm light that illuminated the stone walls. "We did," she replied, a smile breaking through her exhaustion.

But even as they celebrated their victory, a nagging feeling tugged at Elara's mind. "Is it truly over?" she wondered aloud.

Aric nodded, though his eyes held a hint of concern. "I think so, but we should be careful. The darkness may not be gone for good."

"Let's check the altar," Elara said, moving forward cautiously.

As they approached, the remnants of the shattered crystal lay before them, glowing faintly. The symbols carved into the altar pulsed with a soft light, their energy shifting with the rhythm of the cavern.

"Maybe we can use the keys to seal this place," Aric suggested, looking down at the altar. "It might prevent any remnants of the darkness from returning."

Elara nodded, a sense of purpose igniting within her. "Let's do it."

They stepped forward, placing the keys on the altar. As they did, the symbols began to glow brightly, intertwining with the keys' magic. A wave of energy surged through the cavern, and Elara felt a deep connection to the very heart of the citadel.

"Together," she murmured, glancing at Aric. "Let's seal it once and for all."

As they focused their magic into the keys, the altar responded, drawing upon the energy of the cavern. The light expanded, enveloping them in a cocoon of warmth, and for a brief moment, Elara felt an overwhelming sense of peace.

But in that moment of tranquility, she couldn't shake the feeling that their fight was far from over. The shadows might be vanquished for now, but a new chapter awaited them, one that would test their bond and their resolve like never before

Chapter 22: A Flicker of Hope

As the light enveloped Elara and Aric, a calm washed over them, dispelling the remnants of fear that had lingered in the wake of their battle. The keys pulsed rhythmically with the energy of the citadel, weaving their magic into the fabric of the altar.

With a final surge of power, the altar erupted in a blinding flash, sealing the darkness within the depths of the cavern. The light washed over the stone walls, illuminating ancient runes and symbols long hidden by shadows.

Elara felt a deep connection to the citadel, an ancient bond forged through their fight against the darkness. "It's working!" she exclaimed, her heart soaring with hope.

Aric stood beside her, a look of awe on his face. "We're really doing it," he said, a smile breaking through the exhaustion.

As the light began to fade, Elara noticed something glimmering in the corner of her vision. A small, ethereal figure emerged from the shadows, flitting towards them. It was a spirit, its form shimmering like mist in the sunlight.

"Thank you, brave ones," the spirit said, its voice soft and melodic. "You have saved this place from eternal darkness."

"Who are you?" Elara asked, her curiosity piqued.

"I am the Guardian Spirit of the Citadel," it replied, its features becoming clearer. "For ages, I have watched over this land, bound by the balance of light and dark. You have restored that balance and freed me from the shadows."

"What can we do to help?" Aric asked, his expression earnest.

"Your courage and unity have already made a difference," the spirit replied, floating closer. "But the journey is not yet complete. The remnants of the darkness may linger, seeking to regain their power."

Elara felt a shiver run down her spine. "What do we need to do?"

"The darkness is drawn to fear and despair. You must confront it wherever it manifests, and unite the Fire Hunters once more," the spirit urged. "Only then can you ensure lasting peace."

Aric nodded, determination shining in his eyes. "We'll gather the Hunters and face whatever comes next."

"Remember, your strength lies in your bond," the spirit reminded them. "Do not falter, for the shadows will test you."

With a final nod of gratitude, the spirit shimmered, dissolving into the air like morning mist. Elara and Aric stood in the newly illuminated cavern, the weight of their next mission settling heavily on their shoulders.

"Let's head back," Elara said, taking a deep breath. "We need to warn the others and prepare."

As they retraced their steps through the cavern, the remnants of their battle still resonated in the air, a reminder of the darkness they had faced together. They ascended back through the chasm, the journey feeling shorter now that they carried the hope of the spirit within them.

Emerging into the light of the valley, Elara felt invigorated, ready to rally the Fire Hunters and confront whatever awaited them.

Chapter 23: The Gathering Storm

Back in the valley, the atmosphere was tense, the air thick with uncertainty. Elara and Aric made their way to the Fire Hunters' encampment, the sight of familiar faces bringing a sense of comfort. But as they approached, Elara noticed the worried expressions etched on her fellow Hunters' faces.

"Elara! Aric!" one of the Hunters, Mira, rushed toward them. "We were beginning to worry! What happened down there?"

"We faced the darkness," Elara replied, her voice steady despite the memories of the battle still fresh in her mind. "But it's not over yet. We need to gather everyone; there may be more threats coming our way."

The crowd of Hunters turned their attention to her, the urgency in her voice palpable. "We sealed the source of the darkness in the Abyss," she continued, "but we must unite and prepare for any remnants that may still linger."

Mira nodded, rallying the others. "Let's gather everyone. We'll need to fortify our defenses and share what we know."

As they worked to assemble the Fire Hunters, Elara felt a renewed sense of purpose. Together, they began to share stories of the battle, detailing the darkness they had encountered and the spirit that had offered them guidance.

"We can't let fear take hold," Aric said, addressing the group. "We've faced darkness before, and we've emerged stronger. This time will be no different."

The Hunters nodded, their resolve strengthening as they discussed strategies to safeguard their home. They prepared defenses, setting up barriers of flame and light, ready to repel any darkness that might attempt to breach their newfound peace.

But as night fell, an unsettling calm settled over the valley. Elara stood with Aric on the outskirts of the camp, gazing into the distance where the horizon met the stars.

"Do you think they'll come for us?" Elara asked, her voice barely above a whisper.

"I don't know," Aric replied, his gaze fixed ahead. "But we have to be ready for anything. We've faced the darkness before, and we'll face it again."

Elara took a deep breath, trying to quell the fear that threatened to creep in. "I won't let it take hold," she vowed, determination igniting within her. "We'll protect this place."

As the night deepened, shadows danced at the edges of the campfire's light, and Elara couldn't shake the feeling that something was watching them. The remnants of the darkness were out there, waiting for an opportunity to strike.

With the Fire Hunters assembled and ready, she knew they would face whatever came next together. And as dawn approached, bringing with it the promise of a new day, Elara felt a flicker of hope igniting in her heart, a reminder that as long as they stood united, they could face any challenge that lay ahead

Chapter 24: Shadows Unleashed

The dawn broke over the valley, casting golden light across the encampment. Elara awoke to the sounds of the Fire Hunters preparing for the day, but an uneasy tension hung in the air.

As she stepped out of her tent, she found Aric standing at the edge of the camp, his expression serious as he scanned the horizon. "Anything?" she asked, joining him.

"Just the usual," he replied, but his voice held an undercurrent of concern. "But something feels off. The shadows seem… restless."

Elara nodded, her instincts mirroring his unease. "We need to remain vigilant. The spirit warned us about remnants of the darkness."

The Hunters gathered around a central fire, their faces set with determination. "Today, we fortify our defenses and patrol the perimeter," Elara announced, her voice strong. "We can't afford to let our guard down."

As they prepared, Elara felt a prickling sensation at the back of her neck, an instinct that something was coming. She glanced around the camp, her heart racing.

Suddenly, a piercing howl echoed through the valley, followed by the rustling of leaves and the sound of something massive crashing through the underbrush. The Hunters froze, their weapons drawn, eyes wide with fear.

"Form up!" Aric commanded, positioning himself beside Elara. "Stay together!"

From the shadows of the trees, dark figures began to emerge—twisted forms of shadow and smoke that writhed and pulsed with malevolent energy. Elara's heart sank as she recognized the remnants of the darkness they had fought before.

"Prepare yourselves!" she shouted, summoning her fire magic. Flames ignited at her fingertips, a bright shield against the encroaching shadows.

The darkness surged forward, howling and screeching, eager to reclaim its lost power. The Fire Hunters stood their ground, flames and light illuminating the chaos as they clashed with the shadows.

"Fight back!" Aric yelled, slashing through the nearest shadow creature with his sword. "We've faced worse than this!"

Elara focused her magic, sending waves of fire toward the advancing darkness. Each burst of flame lit up the gloom, pushing back against the shadows. But the creatures were relentless, pouring forth from the woods like a tide.

"Fall back!" Mira shouted, coordinating the retreat. "We need to regroup!"

As the Hunters fell back to a defensible position, Elara felt the weight of fear creeping in. "We can't let them overwhelm us!" she yelled, determination surging through her.

But just as they managed to regain their footing, a figure stepped forward from the shadows—a woman cloaked in darkness, her eyes glinting with a malevolent light.

"You thought you could seal away the darkness?" she taunted, her voice smooth and chilling. "You have merely delayed the inevitable."

"Who are you?" Elara demanded, stepping forward, fire crackling around her.

"I am the Harbinger," the woman replied, her smile sinister. "The darkness you sealed has only grown stronger, and now it will consume you all."

With a wave of her hand, the shadows surged forward with renewed ferocity, and Elara knew they had to act quickly.

"Stand strong!" she cried, rallying her fellow Hunters. "We can't let them take our home!"

Chapter 25: The Final Stand

The battle raged on, the clash of light and darkness echoing through the valley. Elara fought fiercely alongside her comrades, flames roaring around her as she targeted the nearest shadow creature.

"Keep pushing them back!" Aric shouted, slicing through the darkness. "We can't let the Harbinger get close!"

Elara's heart raced as she focused on the swirling shadows. The Harbinger moved gracefully through the chaos, her laughter ringing out like a death knell.

"Your efforts are futile!" she taunted. "You cannot hope to defeat what is already part of you!"

Elara gritted her teeth, pushing back against the despair creeping into her thoughts. "We are not afraid of you!" she shouted, channeling all her energy into a powerful fireball aimed directly at the Harbinger.

But the dark figure merely waved her hand, and the flames dissipated into wisps of smoke. "You'll have to do better than that," she sneered.

Mira stumbled, shadows coiling around her legs. "Help!" she cried, but the darkness threatened to pull her under.

"Hold on!" Aric shouted, rushing toward her. "Elara, cover me!"

Elara nodded, conjuring a wall of fire to protect them as Aric reached for Mira. With a powerful swing of his sword, he severed the shadows binding her, pulling her back into the safety of the circle.

"Thank you," Mira gasped, catching her breath. "But we can't keep this up forever."

Elara felt the weight of her fear creeping in again. "We have to find a way to defeat the Harbinger. If we can disrupt her connection to the darkness, maybe we can turn the tide."

Aric looked around, determination hardening his features. "We'll need to fight together, focus our powers on her."

As they rallied their strength, the Harbinger's laughter echoed through the valley. "You think unity can save you? The darkness is stronger than you can imagine!"

"Together!" Elara called out, feeling the heat of her magic resonate with the others. "We can do this!"

As one, the Fire Hunters channeled their magic, creating a barrier of fire and light that surged toward the Harbinger. The shadows recoiled, and Elara felt the power of their unity ignite her spirit.

"Now!" she cried, pushing forward as they unleashed their combined energy.

The light blazed, illuminating the valley as it struck the Harbinger, forcing her to stagger back. Shadows writhed around her, but the fire was relentless.

"No!" the Harbinger shrieked, her voice filled with rage and disbelief. "This cannot be!"

With one final push, the Hunters surged forward, enveloping the Harbinger in a vortex of flames and light. The shadows twisted and screamed, collapsing into nothingness as the Harbinger's form disintegrated before their eyes.

The darkness that had plagued them began to recede, the valley breathing a sigh of relief as light flooded the space once more.

Exhausted but triumphant, Elara looked around at her comrades, their faces lit with victory.

"We did it," she breathed, a sense of disbelief washing over her.

"Together," Aric said, a smile breaking through the exhaustion.

Chapter 26: A New Dawn

As the first rays of dawn broke over the horizon, the valley glowed with renewed life. The darkness that had threatened them had been vanquished, and a sense of peace settled over the encampment.

Elara stood with Aric, watching as the Fire Hunters began to rebuild, their spirits lifted. The remnants of the shadows had faded, leaving behind a brighter future.

"We've come so far," Elara said, her heart swelling with pride. "I never would have made it without you and the others."

Aric smiled, his eyes shining with warmth. "We're a team. We've faced darkness together, and we'll face whatever comes next together too."

As they looked out over the valley, Elara felt a flicker of hope igniting within her. The spirit's words echoed in her mind, reminding her of the strength they had found in unity.

"I think this is just the beginning," she said, determination returning to her voice. "We need to protect this place, make sure the darkness never returns."

"And we will," Aric replied. "We'll gather the Fire Hunters, train, and strengthen our bonds."

With a renewed sense of purpose, Elara turned back to the camp, ready to lead her comrades into a new era. The darkness might have been defeated, but their fight for balance and light was just beginning.

As the sun rose higher in the sky, casting warmth over the valley, Elara knew that no matter the challenges ahead, they would face them together. The bonds they had forged through their trials would guide them, illuminating their path as they embraced the dawn of a new day—a day of hope, unity, and resilience.

And as the first flowers bloomed in the valley, Elara felt a promise in the air—a promise that as long as they stood together, light would always prevail over darkness.

Printed in Great Britain
by Amazon